PUFFIN BOOKS

**Shark Island**

Angie Sage lives in Bristol and has two daughters aged twelve and seventeen. She studied illustration at Leicester Polytechnic and since then has illustrated many children's books. She started writing eight years ago and now writes and illustrates for ages three to ten. When Angie Sage is not writing or drawing, she likes walking along a Cornish beach and watching the sea.

# SHARK ISLAND

## ANGIE SAGE

PUFFIN BOOKS

*For Luke, who swims faster than any penguin*

PUFFIN BOOKS

Published by the Penguin Group
Penguin Books Ltd, 27 Wrights Lane, London W8 5TZ, England
Penguin Books USA Inc., 375 Hudson Street, New York, New York 10014, USA
Penguin Books Australia Ltd, Ringwood, Victoria, Australia
Penguin Books Canada Ltd, 10 Alcorn Avenue, Toronto, Ontario, Canada M4V 3B2
Penguin Books (NZ) Ltd, 182–190 Wairau Road, Auckland 10, New Zealand

Penguin Books Ltd, Registered Offices: Harmondsworth, Middlesex, England

First published 1997
10 9 8 7 6 5 4 3 2 1

Copyright © Angie Sage, 1997
All rights reserved

The moral right of the author/illustrator has been asserted

Made and printed in England by Clays Ltd, St Ives plc

British Library Cataloguing in Publication Data
A CIP catalogue record for this book is available from the British Library

ISBN 0–140–38120–1

One bright, sunny day in Penguin Bay, when all the penguins were busy catching fish for their supper, the Giant Squid arrived.

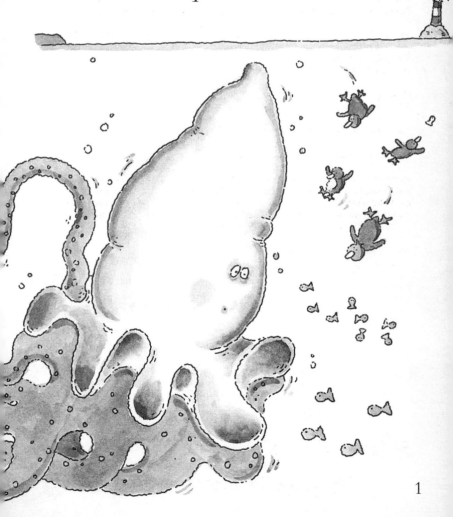

1

Great-uncle Penk, his nephew
Penk, and all Penk's friends
watched it swim in.
"Look at that!"
"What?"
"That!"
"Where?"
"There, silly."

What is it?

"That," said Great-uncle Penk
solemnly, "is the Giant Squid."

The Giant Squid settled down happily in Penguin Bay.

Ah, peace and quiet at last

But soon it had eaten all the
fish in Penguin Bay and had
nearly eaten a few penguins (by
mistake).

The Giant Squid may have been happy, but the penguins were not.

The penguins were hungry. They looked everywhere for fish, but they found nothing, not even a tiddler.

7

But it wasn't Penk's tummy
rumbling, it was thunder.

That night, there was a storm.

When the penguins woke up the
next morning, there was something
else in Penguin Bay.

"Oh no, it's another giant
squid!" gasped Penk.

Great-uncle Penk looked
through his telescope.

9

So every morning a penguin rowed out to the crate, and came back with a boat full of bananas.

All afternoon the penguins sat
on the rocks, eating bananas and
talking about fish.

"What about those little fish
with the pointy noses?"
"Oh, yum!"

But when it was Penk's turn to row out and fetch the bananas, something awful happened. The storm came back.

The thunder crashed and the lightning flashed.

Penk hid underneath fifty-six bananas in the bottom of the boat while the wind howled and blew him all the way to Shark Island.

13

The first thing that Penk saw
when he dared to poke his head
up from under the bananas was
Slasher Shark. The second thing
that Penk saw was Sluggit Shark.

"There's a tasty penguin in that boat, Sluggit," said Slasher.

"Yeah. Let's get him," said Sluggit.

15

Slasher and Sluggit Shark were fast swimmers. They were even faster swimmers when they were chasing a tasty penguin.

"SNAP, SNAP, CRASH!"

The tasty penguin's boat fell to pieces and the tasty penguin flew through the air, followed by fifty-six bananas.

THUMP!

The tasty penguin landed on
Shark Island, and the bananas
landed on the tasty penguin.

18

Slasher and Sluggit crashed into
a rock and banged their noses.

"We'll get that penguin,
Sluggit," said Slasher.

"Yeah. We'll get him," said
Sluggit.

Penk sat on the beach on Shark Island and looked at the sea. He was longing to jump in and catch a fresh, juicy fish, but he knew that there were two big fish in there waiting to catch *him*.

Penk sighed and peeled a banana.

When Penk had finished his banana he decided to collect some pebbles. Penk laid out the pebbles very carefully along the sand so that they spelt "HELP".

Then he stood on a big rock and looked out to sea.

He was looking for the Penguin Rescue Ship.

The Penguin Rescue Ship was a rescue ship full of penguins. Its captain was Great-uncle Penk.

The day after the storm, the Penguin Rescue Ship sailed out of Penguin Bay, but it was not looking for Penk.

It was towing away the Giant Squid. The Giant Squid did not want to be towed away.

Oi, get off. I want to stay in Penguin Bay!

"No! You've eaten all our fish and now you've eaten poor little Penk *and* his boat. You are *not* staying."

"But I didn't eat Penk," said the Giant Squid. "And I certainly didn't eat his boat. I would have remembered eating a *boat*."

Great-uncle Penk did not believe him.

The Penguin Rescue Ship sailed on past the Penguin Lighthouse.

"Where are you taking me?" asked the Giant Squid.

"Back to where you came from," said Great-uncle Penk. "Back to Shark Island."

"No!" said the Giant Squid. "I am not going back to Shark Island. Not while Slasher and Sluggit are there."

The Giant Squid wrapped a huge tentacle around the Penguin Lighthouse.

"I am staying here," it said.

27

The Penguin Rescue Ship pulled
and pulled but it could not move
the Giant Squid.

The lighthouse penguins looked out to see what was going on.

"Get off the lighthouse!"

"No!"

"I know what to do," said one of them. "This always works." He went and fetched a feather duster and tickled the Giant Squid.

"He-he-he! No, *stoppit!*" giggled the Giant Squid.

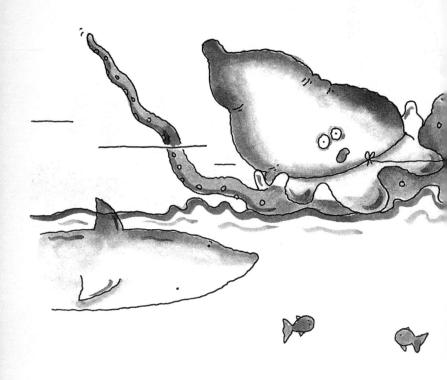

The Giant Squid let go of the
lighthouse and the Penguin Rescue
Ship shot out to sea, faster than
any Penguin Rescue Ship had ever
gone before.

It was going so fast that it even
overtook Doris Shark.

Doris was out looking for her
twins, Slasher and Sluggit Shark,
who had swum away from school
and had not come back.

The Penguin Rescue Ship and the Giant Squid sped over the sea.

It was not long before they reached Shark Island.

Penk saw them coming. He waved his flippers and jumped up and down, up and down, up and WHOOSH – Penk slipped on the banana skin. He skidded straight off the rock and tumbled into the sea. SPLASH!

33

"It's that penguin again,
Sluggit," said Slasher.

"Yeah. Let's get him," said
Sluggit.

34

Slasher and Sluggit loomed up
in front of Penk. They grinned
huge, toothy grins and opened
their mouths very wide.

Penk had never seen so many
sharp pointy teeth in his life.

The next moment Penk was
flying through the air as Slasher
and Sluggit played "Catch the
Penguin". They threw Penk higher
and higher.

"I'll have the top half and you
have the bottom half, Sluggit,"
said Slasher.

"That's not fair. *You* have the
bottom half," said Sluggit.

On the Penguin Rescue Ship, Great-uncle Penk looked through his telescope.

He saw Shark Island. He saw a sign on the beach saying "HELP".

Then he saw a flying penguin.

"It's Penk!" shouted Great-uncle Penk."Full steam ahead."

The Penguin Rescue Ship steamed off to do what it did best – rescue a penguin. It was not long before it steamed up to Slasher and Sluggit Shark.

"Put that penguin down!" shouted Great-uncle Penk to Slasher and Sluggit.

Slasher and Sluggit took no notice. They carried on playing "Catch the Penguin".

"Help!" shouted Penk.

41

Great-uncle Penk knew what to do.

"Penguins to the rescue!" he shouted. All the penguins in the Penguin Rescue Ship jumped into the water and started swimming towards Slasher and Sluggit Shark.

But far below them glided a dark shark-shape. It was Doris Shark.

Doris Shark was cross. She had
spent weeks looking for Slasher
and Sluggit, but they were
nowhere to be found.

Doris Shark was hungry too.

Then she looked up through the
water and saw hundreds of chewy
little penguin feet paddling
through the water.

"Yum," thought Doris Shark.

Doris Shark sped up, up, up
through the water as fast as a
hungry shark can go.

"SNAP, SNAP, SNAP," went
Doris's teeth, but before she could
snap up even a tiny pair of
penguin feet, something very
strange happened to Doris Shark.

Doris Shark went flying.

The Giant Squid had grabbed hold of Doris and lifted her right up out of the sea.

"You leave them penguins alone," said the Giant Squid. "You sharks are nothing but a nuisance. Look at those two troublemakers over there."

Doris looked at Slasher and Sluggit. Slasher and Sluggit looked at Doris.

"Hello, Mum," they said.

"What do you two think you are doing?" demanded Doris. "I've been looking for you everywhere. You are both coming straight home."

"Yes, Mum," said Slasher and Sluggit.

"Are you taking them home now?" asked the Giant Squid.

"Yes," said Doris.

"Right now?"

"Yes," said Doris, "right now."

"Good," said the Giant Squid, and he dropped Doris Shark back into the sea.

SPLASH!

Doris swam over to Slasher and Sluggit.

"Put that penguin down," she said crossly. "You are both coming straight home with me."

"Yes, Mum."

Slasher and Sluggit put that penguin down.

The rescue penguins swam out
to Penk and brought him back to
the Penguin Rescue Ship.

They all watched happily as
Doris, Slasher and Sluggit Shark
swam off into the distance.

Bye-bye
sharks!

The Penguin Rescue Ship towed the Giant Squid around Shark Island to its favourite part of the sea bed. It was very pleased to be back.

There's no place like home

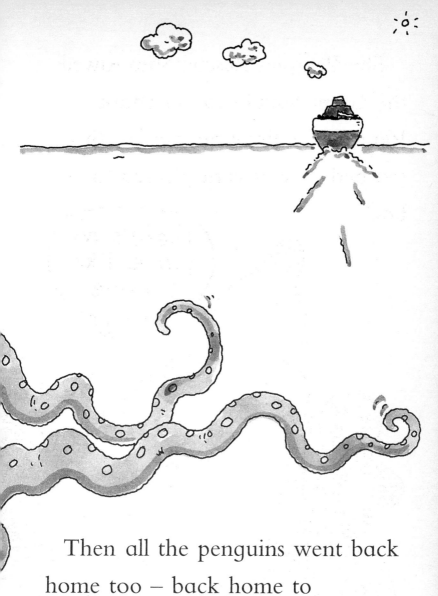

Then all the penguins went back
home too – back home to
Penguin Bay.

The Penguin Rescue Ship sailed into Penguin Bay past the crate of bananas.

Eurgh!

Penk was the first one to jump into the water. He dived down into the cool blue sea and caught a fish. It was his favourite – a big, fat fish with green spots.

The fish were back in Penguin Bay, and so were all the penguins. And they never ever ate a banana again.